My Dad THiNKS He's Funny

My Dad THiNKS He's Funny

Katrina Germein

illustrated by **Tom Jellett**

CANDLEWICK PRESS

My dad thinks he's funny.

Whenever I say,
"I'm hungry,"
Dad says,

"Hello,
Hungry.
Pleased
to meet
you."

Whenever I put lots of
ketchup on my plate,
Dad says,

"Would
you like
some
dinner
with
that
ketchup?"

And whenever we're about to cut up a cake for dessert, Dad says,
"Well, there's my piece. What's everyone else having?"

the eye roll

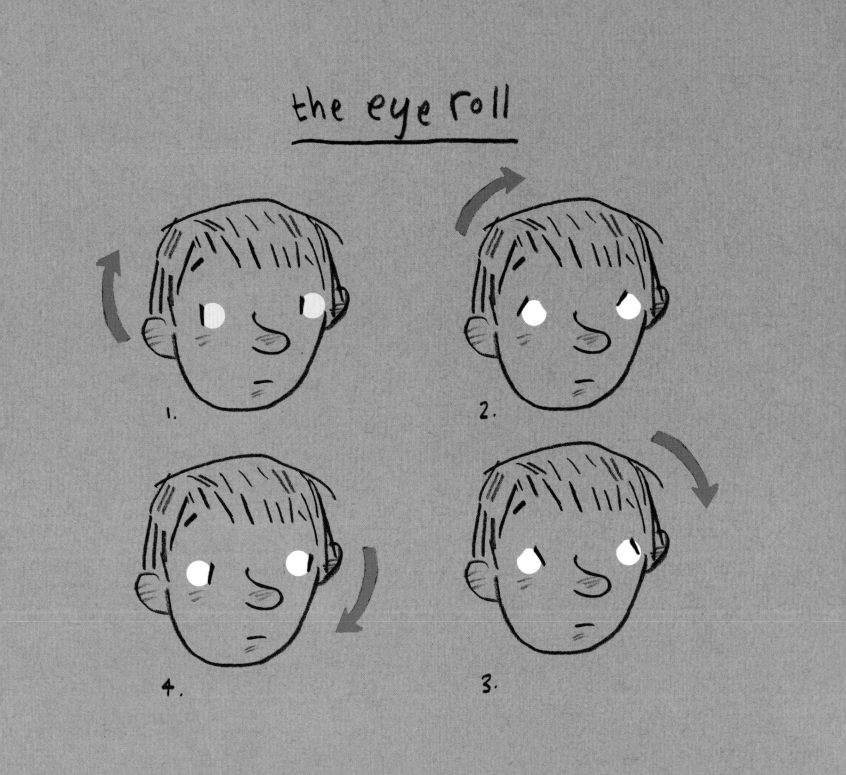

My dad thinks he's funny.

When I say, "Dad, do you know what?" He says, "I don't know What, but I know his brother."

When I say, "Dad, I don't know how," he says, "I know How. He's What's brother."

And when I say, "Dad, I don't want to," he says,

"Okay, then . . . Do you want three?"

My dad thinks he's funny.

When I tell Dad my finger hurts, he says,

"Let's chop it off!"

When I tell Dad my foot hurts, he says,

"No problem. You've got another."

And when I tell Dad I think there's something
in my eye, he says,

"Yeah, an eyeball."

My dad thinks he's funny.

If anyone asks,

"How is it going?" Dad says,

"By bus."

If I fall, Dad says,

"Welcome home.
How was your trip?"

And if anyone asks,

"What's up?"
Dad says,

"Just the sky."

My dad thinks he's funny.

When people say,
"How are you feeling?"
Dad says,
"With my hands."

When people say,
"Would you like sugar?"

And when Dad says,

"Time for a special announcement,"

we leave the room fast,
before it really
starts to smell.

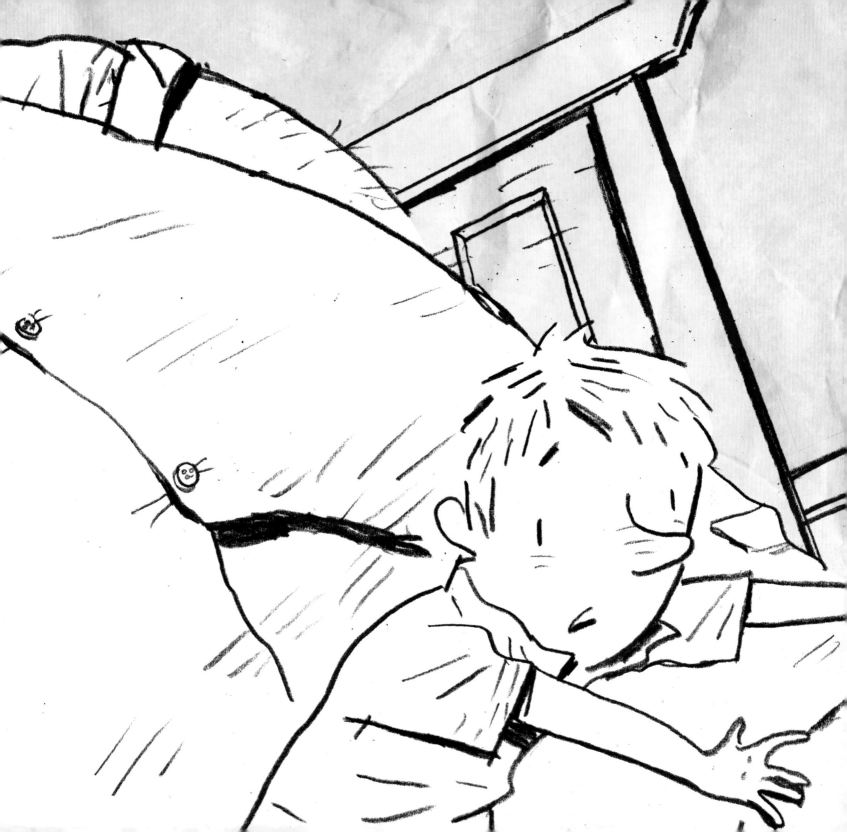

My dad
thinks
he's funny.

Sometimes, he
stands in front of
the television.
"Dad," I say, "I can't see."

**"Well, open
your eyes,"** he says.

My dad thinks he's funny.

Whenever I go swimming, Dad says,
"Try not to get wet!"

Whenever I go shopping, Dad says,
"Buy me some money!"

And whenever I say I'm going
to the bathroom, Dad says,
"Don't get lost!"

My dad thinks he's funny.

When Mom says, "How did your day go?"

Dad says, **"It didn't go anywhere. I had to push it."**

When Mom says, "I'm just going to jump in the shower," Dad says, **"That sounds dangerous."**

And when Mom says,
"The neighbors' garden is
looking pretty" . . .

Dad says, **"Yeah, pretty *strange*."**

My dad thinks he's funny.

My dad thinks he's funny.

When I ask Dad
for a hand, he says,

"Which one
do you want,
left or right?"

At bedtime when I ask Dad if I
can stay up late, he says,

"Not tonight.
But you can
last night."

When Mom says to me,
"Come and give me a kiss,
gorgeous," Dad says,

"I'll be right there."

My dad thinks he's funny.

"Good night," I say when Dad
tucks me in.

"Good
morning,"

Dad says.

Then he pulls the
covers over my head,

kisses my feet,

and turns on the light.

My dad
THiNKS he's
funny!

For the dads — Grant, Honi, Steve, and Alan, with lots of love
K. G.

For Alfie, Charlie, and Tian Tian
T. J.

First U.S. edition 2013

Library of Congress Catalog Card Number 2012947248
ISBN 978-0-7636-6522-7

SCP 18 17 16 15 14 13
10 9 8 7 6 5 4 3 2 1

Printed in Humen, Dongguan, China

This book was typeset in Klepto ITC.
The illustrations were done in mixed media.

Candlewick Press
99 Dover Street
Somerville, Massachusetts 02144

visit us at www.candlewick.com